Once Upon a Garden

Sophie's Shell

Jo Rooks

MAGINATION PRESS ❧ WASHINGTON, DC
American Psychological Association

For Tayla and David

With special thanks to Christyan. —*JR*

Books for Kids From the
American Psychological Association

Magination Press is a registered trademark of the American
Psychological Association. Order books at maginationpress.org
or call 1-800-374-2721.

Book design by Gwen Grafft

Printed by Lake Book Manufacturing, Inc.

Library of Congress Cataloging-in-Publication Data
Names: Rooks, Jo, author, illustrator.
Title: Sophie's shell / by Jo Rooks.
Description: Washington, D.C. : Magination Press, [2019] |
  Series: [Once upon a garden] | "American Psychological
  Association." | Summary: Sophie the snail, eager to start
  school and have her many questions answered, is overcome
  by shyness and keeps popping into her shell until a new
  friend helps.
Identifiers: LCCN 2018046766| ISBN 9781433830891
  (hardcover) | ISBN 1433830892 (hardcover)
Subjects: | CYAC: First day of school—Fiction. | Schools—
  Fiction. | Bashfulness—Fiction. | Snails—Fiction. |
  Animals—Fiction.
Classification: LCC PZ7.1.R66854 Sop 2019 | DDC [E]—
  dc23 LC record available at https://lccn.loc.gov/2018046766

Manufactured in the United States of America
10 9 8 7 6 5 4 3 2 1

This is Sophie.

Sophie **loved** learning about the world
and was always pondering **BIG questions** like …

"Why is the sky blue?"

"Why are raindrops wet?"

"Where does the sun go at the end of the day?"

And … what are stars made of?

Sophie couldn't wait to start school
where she could find out the answers
to all her questions.

And finally, that day **arrived!**

Sophie was so excited!

But when she reached the school gates, she felt a
wobbly feeling in her tummy.

"Come meet the class," said Miss Flutterby.

But Sophie felt shy. **Too shy** to say hello.

When suddenly…

POP!

"Oh dear," thought Sophie.

In art class, Sophie painted a **big** picture.
"That's beautiful!" said Beatrice.

Sophie felt shy. **Too shy** to reply. **When ...**

POP!

"Not again," thought Sophie.

At lunchtime, Sophie had all her favorite things.

"What have you got?" asked Layla.

Sophie felt shy. **Too shy** to talk to Layla.

Then ...

"Why do I feel so shy?"

Sophie asked herself from inside her shell.

Then, a voice replied. "Sometimes, I feel shy too."

Sophie wasn't sure where the voice came from …

so

she

peeped

out.

"Want to hear a joke?" said Stanley.

Stanley told Sophie so many jokes that
their shells shook with giggles.

After lunch, it was time for "show-and-tell."

William showed the class the gold
coin he had found.

Lucy told everyone about
her special award.

And Stanley wanted to
tell a joke.

Everyone waited ...

but Stanley didn't say **anything.**

Oh, no! Had Stanley forgotten his own joke?
Then ...

POP!

Poor Stanley!

Somehow, Sophie felt brave. She knew **exactly** what to do.
She took a deep breath and slowly slid to the front.

"Sometimes, I feel shy too," she said to the class.
"But having a friend like Stanley is the **best** remedy ever."

"Want to hear a joke?" said Stanley with a big smile.

"What did the **BIG** flower say to the **little** flower?"
asked Stanley.
"We don't know," chanted the class.
"What **did** the **BIG** flower say to the **little** flower?"

"What's up, Bud!"

They replied together.

Everyone **loved** the joke
and thought they made
a **great** double act!

After that, Sophie liked making **new** friends.

But she knew that her shell was always there ...

just in case she ever needed it.